THE RATTY RACERS

Maddy McClellan

For my
beautiful boys
Inigo and Rafael

First published in 2012
by Meadowside Children's Books

This edition published in 2018 by Albury Books
Albury Court, Albury, Thame, Oxfordshire
OX9 2LP, United Kingdom

www.AlburyBooks.com

Text & Illustrations © Maddy McClellan 2012

The right of Maddy McClellan to be identified
as the author and illustrator of this work has
been asserted by her in accordance with the
Copyright, Designs and Patents Act, 1988

A CIP catalogue record for this book
is available from the British Library

For orders:
Kuperard Publishers and Distributors
+44 (0) 2084462440 | office@kuperard.co.uk

isbn: 978-1-910571-18-7

Printed in Turkey

Albury Books

Rosie Rat lived on a rubbish heap
with her friends. They were very happy.
People threw away all kinds of
fascinating things.

One day, Rosie looked at her friends scampering about, playing amongst the odds and ends, making clever creations and ingenious inventions... and it gave her a **brilliant idea!**

"Let's have a Ratty Recycling Race!
We'll get into teams and see
what we can make!"

The rats whiffled their whiskers in excitement
and scurried straight to work.

They **hammered**
and **nailed**,

tied
and
glued,
bent
and
fitted,

built and even **knitted**
until each team had made...

an excellent and elaborate,
fancy and **extravagant**...

Ratty Racing Machine!

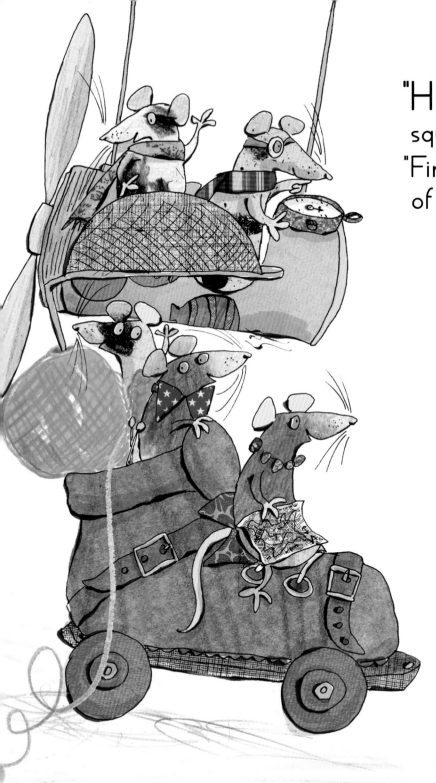

"How thrilling!"
squeaked Rosie.
"First team to the end
of town is the winner!

On your marks,
get set, **go!**

Let the
Rat Race
begin!"

Felix and Florence were off in a flash...

Whoosh!

Clarence and Cristabel cruised off ahead...

Weeeeeee!

Ginger and Jonesy
jetted to the front...

WHIZZ!

Bluebell and Bernie
burst into the lead...

ZOOM!

Only Cyril and Sophie made a slow start
as they sailed along silently under the drains.

But then Felix
and Florence jolted

and halted!

Ginger and Jonesy

heaved and huffed!

Clarence and Cristabel ducked and **dodged**!

Bluebell and Bernie got distracted...

and then got terribly **tangled!**
But where were Cyril
and Sophie?

Now the Ratty Racers are rapidly approaching!

Ginger and Jonesy are hurtling along, clattering and **rattling...**

Bluebell and Bernie are close behind whirling **and twirling...**

Clarence and Cristabel
are rocketing past,
recklessly rapid
**and honking
the hooter!**

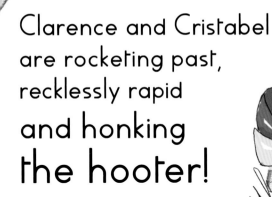

Now Felix and Florence
and Rosie Rat too, fly out
in a flurry, **faster and
faster!**

The finish is in sight, but then...

Clattering! Confusion! Chaos! COLLISION!

With a mix and a muddle and a tangle of tails, the Ratty Racers are hurled in a heap!

Cyril and Sophie have sprung up from below!
They've won by a whisker!

The Ratty Racers all giggle with glee!

And Rosie, resplendent, rejoices in raptures.

"What a rollicking rackety
Ratty Rat Race!"

Make your own Ratty Racing Boat!

You will need...
- Milk/orange juice carton
- Small cardboard box
- Scrap paper
- Straw
- Scissors
- Glue
- Tape
- String

1. Cut the carton in half.
(You may need a grown-up to help you do this.)

2. Make a hole in the side of the small cardboard box and then glue it inside the carton.

3. Make a little hole through the top of the straw.

4. Cut out a piece of paper and make two holes in the middle, one at the top and one at the bottom.

5. Thread the straw through the holes in the paper and then push the straw into the hole in the small box.

6. Thread the string through the hole in the straw and attach each end to the top and bottom of the carton with tape.

7. Ta-da! You're ready to sail your Ratty Racing Boat!